XXXPLEASURES:
WET KISSES

christopher mainor

follow me on twitter @chrismainor
Christopher@christophermainor.com

JACE MEDIA

New Jersey | New York

Cover Design by JACE MEDIA

Typeset by JACE MEDIA

Library of Congress Cataloging-in-Publication data
(to follow)

ISBM 978-0615592282 (paper)
1. XXXPLEASURES: WET KISSES

Printed in the Great State of New Jersey of the
United States of America.

~deep up in you stroking and forcing all of me inside you, I clutch your neck and squeeze with enough sensuality that my body movement gets more intense

feeling your breathing getting heavier as it hits the right side of my face, your hands grasp my hips to command my movements to assist your body with its expulsion of sexual secretions

with you pressed up against the bedroom door with nowhere to go, your legs wrapped around me, I dig deeper and thrust harder. Enchanted by the way my love muscle is working, you give way to your stream of liquescent river flowing from between your thighs~

XXXPLEASURES: WET KISSES

Table of Moistness

Couples Massage

Sitting in the lobby draped in white plush robes sipping on glasses of water with lemon wedges, we converse about how this night is going to end. Smiling from ear to ear you let it be known that this is something you would have never imagined just out of the blue.

A small Asian lady appears and tells us to follow her; she leads us to a private secluded room with candles lit, soft music playing and two massage tables with crisp white linen. Closing the door as we enter, we kiss and fondle each other, almost getting caught up in the passion. Suddenly there is a knock at the door, and two ladies come in and motion for us to lay down on our perspective tables.

The couples massage is well under way as they massage, caress, and knead the stress of our bodies out. Feeling stress free and physically refreshed as well as sexually motivated, you reach out your hand to grab mine. Holding hands while getting the kinks worked out, your senses are getting heightened and excited with lust.

After the ladies leave the room for us to get dressed, I sit up and just stare at you in all your beauty. Joining you on your table I lay my body on top of yours, loving the feel of your skin so close to mine. Feeling my erection pierce through your inner thighs you open your eyes and turn your head. Placing my hands on top of yours, you tighten your fingers. Sticking your butt up to embrace me it with all its glory you feel the tip of my head touch the opening of your lips.

As the head touches you, your body let's out some sweet secretions making your opening even more acceptable for penetration. Raising your hips to force a pleasurable entry I meet you with a gentle push forward, The face you make as the head enters is priceless. Moving forward til I am deep within your walls you start to gyrate them lovely hips to engulf my dick with your body and juices.

My legs split yours in the middle as I lay on you. Our actions become more pronounced as we get in the groove. Your moans and movement take over the room as I drive harder, longer and deeper; your grip on my hands get tighter and tighter. Feeling the urge you lean backwards to the doggy position.

Without missing a beat we continue to fuck like never before.

In this position, I brace your hips with my left hand and grab your hair with my right hand. Pulling back to make the back of your head touch your back I swerve and swirl; I pull out til the head is just touching, then I push it back in to swerve and swirl again and again. With an arch in your back and your sweet heart shaped ass propped up just right, each stroke is felt the way it is meant to feel. With the driving force of a Mack truck each motion is delivered on point and on time.

Pulling your hair while I am taking care of business, you fall into a sublimed blissful state of paradise. Your body starts to shake as your inner thighs clamp up and grip my thick pulsating dick is digging deep. Letting out several moans, I feel your body as it is talking to me. Reaching my right hand around your body I grab your throat and squeeze with just enough pressure to stifle your moans, but also take you over to the edge and over the climactic peak. Your body gives way to an ultimate orgasm that takes total control over you in pure seduction. Fighting hard to regain control you bite your lip, but that will power is broken as your body exerts full control and your juices flow from you like a water hydrant in the summer!

Realizing you lost the battle, you just relax in my arms as your quivering arms and shaking legs dominate you. No fear, I have you wrapped up in my arms, my warm embrace, my sensual touch and caressing hands.

As soon as your sensual explosion subsides, I turn you over and smile as I look at your wonderful body, a work of art! Backing up and into position, I quickly jump right into the mission at hand; to lick you like you never have been licked before. With my arms on top of your thighs I push back the hood on your clit and proceed to lick it, and just as I go to stick my tongue into you, I use my left thumb to tease your clit. Thumbing it and the feeling of my tongue got you squirting out lil puffs of moisture all over my tongue. Just so you know, I like when you do that thing, the way your body just lets go and pushes out your sweet nectar like secretions.

Getting full of your juices, I can feel your right leg probing under my body and touching my dick. With your toes you feel that it is getting harder with every touch you are giving it with every squirt you are putting in my mouth.

Grabbing my head with your hands, you caress and then grip and pull in as my tongue holds your clit hostage. With your clit in my mouth, and my chin pointing in your sweetness, I am hitting you with a double dose, a lot of sucking with a minimal amount of penetration pressure.

Feeling your body releasing without your control, it takes over you. As hard as you try to fight it you feel it coming out any way, trying to get away, you start to back peddle til your upper body is off the table. Not letting you get away, I don't let up, I continue to bury my face in you with striking licks and suction like sucking. Feeling your body going over the table, I grip your thighs and start to pull you back up and on the table.

Getting you back on the table as I continue to feast from your beauty; as you wrap those legs around me and clamp down just right. Those luscious thighs feel so right with my arms underneath you doubled back in a controlling position. There is no more running away from this tongue anymore!

Coming up for air, never missing a beat, I roll you onto your side and I come up behind you with my dick in my hand. I line it up with your body and push into you as you raise your leg to give me complete access. With you being so wet, my dick slides in very easily. Way past the head, more than half of the shaft is in now. As you toot your back towards me I pump my body forward. With sweat forming everywhere, our bodies slide across each other with ease. Reaching back you grab my body and pull me into you with every thrust I make. With my arms around you, we make love as if we were married for years. Like I know every inch of your body, we make love like it was the greatest thing in the world.

Holding you close and tight as you continue to push and buck your juicy ass back on me and I continue to push my dick in you balls deep, til we both start to shake as more fluids are expelled.

As your body releases all it had to offer, I slowly pull out of you and I just sit behind you watching as our natural juices ooze out of you and on the sheets on the table, oh what a sight to see!!! Seeing my dick still leaking, you sit up and lean forward taking me in your mouth making sure you get everything I have to give. As you lick up and down my shaft and then make my dick disappear within the walls of your mouth I lay back in total delight. With my arms folded back holding my body up, I feel a shaking in my leg, this shaking came all the way up until it was spewing out me deep into your mouth and down your throat. Ohhh the feeling is so heaven sent. As my body puts out another load and your mouth catches it I lose myself in astonishment at the skills your are proudly presenting in front on me. The way your hand are gripping my thighs, the way you are moving your mouth, the way you are moving your tongue around my shaft has me yearning for more.

But sensing how much time went by since the massage ladies left, after my second shot into your mouth, I lay you back down. Pat you on your pretty ass and grab your towel.

As I cover you up and go back to my table, the lil Asian ladies return with glasses of water, right on time!

Sitting up and sipping on your water, all you can do is look at me with them big beautiful brown eyes of sexual pleasure.

Flexible

Saturday morning I wake up to the sound of the shower running. Thinking to myself, damn, what time is it? I slowly roll out of bed and make my way to the bathroom where I find you stepping into the shower. The shower must be nice and hot as the steam coming from it got the whole bathroom fogged up.

In-between brushing my teeth and washing my face, I sneak peeks of you in the shower through the cloudy shower glass. As the water cascades down your pretty skin, as it ripples over your breast and fall off the cliff hanger of an ass, oh my, I am getting excited just watching you in the shower.

All of a sudden you notice a figure coming into the shower with you. Making room for me, I enter and just hold you as the water dances down your skin and splashes up on mine. Like a kid in the candy store, I reach out to touch you where the water is streaming down over your left breast.

You look me directly into my eyes and tell me, "watch the hair boy!" But as if I wasn't even focused, I continue to just touch your body. With my right hand placed on your left hip I pull your body in closer to mine. As your body presses up against me, you feel my dick named "Fatboy" poking against you. Reaching down you grab him in your hands and start to play with him. Squeezing your breast, I lean in and start kissing and sucking on your pointing nipple as the water runs down and smacks me in the face.

Feeling me getting excited, you reach lower and massage my balls with a gentle touch. I move over to the other breast and go back to kissing and sucking with water all in my face. With my left hand I feel your wet pussy and start touching your clit with forceful circles and rubbing. Hearing you moan is a wonderful thing, to hear your lil dainty voice get a lil bit higher.

In between the moans you start to bite your lip.

With the tip of my tongue I follow the water and gravity and go down. As I am kissing on your belly button, I position your left leg to be perched up on the edge of the shower like a step. Grabbing your pretty round ass with both of my hands, I am completely on my knees and got my face buried in your love canal. Standing up while bending your back to the shower wall, kissing and sucking on your hooded pearl tongue. Using my tongue, I push your clitoris hood back and expose your sweetness to the water running down your body and to my tongue moving it into position. Cocking your legs open more, I grab your clit in my mouth and perform several lil tricks on it while I have it pinned down. Sucking on such a sweet and succulent clit sends you into frenzy, and when I release it, your body shutters a lil bit. Then while licking around it in both clock wise and counter clockwise motions, I feel your hands grip and hold on to my head. With my hands strongly massaging your ass, and my tongue licking your sweets, you drop down an inch trying to put my face inside of you more.

As your body starts to climb your peak, I go back to my sucking and licking routine with an added twist of inserting a finger into you. Probing your insides with my middle finger, I can clearly tell the difference between shower water and your sticky juices. Letting out some very loud silent moans, I feel your juices flowing into my mouth more now. Feeding me with your good vitamin juices, I continue and continue to massage your ass, to suck and lick with my finger still probing your body.

Pulling me up, I slowly pull my finger out of you and come up while letting the water rinse off my face of your juices. Kissing and licking your body on my journey up, I tease and play with both your breast. Coming up and being face to face, we lock lips with the passion of timeless love! Feeling the passion being delivered, you tilt your body over about 2inches to the left as you grab my dick and put the head to your lips. As I push to enter your pussy, you close your eyes and lick your lips.

With a quarter of me in, your body starts to speak about how good it feels. Your nails are sharp as they pierce my shoulders with the tight grip you got them in.

Pushing in deeper and blocking out the pain we get into a rhythm of making love. With the water still running, it feels like we are in the tropics somewhere getting it in under a waterfall. Reaching under you crossing your back, I hold you tight as we continue to do what we weredoing, pulling you down with every thrust I make going up. Digging down low, I make every movement count!

This loving is getting so good I can feel your right leg wrap around and hook me for stability. With my right hand I reach up higher and grab your hair and tug tightly; tight enough to bend your head back some as I keep fucking you as the water splashes all in my face.

As your grip gets tighter and your embrace gets stronger, I can feel your sweetness let loose more juices in a steady flow. Holding you tight, I catch you as your drained body almost collapses. Just standing there motionless, I let you regain your composure then ask if you are ok. Before I get out of the water

As I leave, you tap me on the butt and say, "good morning".

As you come out the shower wrapped up in a milk white towel, I just stand in the bedroom door looking at you. Looking back at the shower you mention, "Wasn't that shower steaming hot when we got in?, Now it is ice cold. Damn boy!!" As you walk past me into the bedroom I snatch off the towel quick as hell. You just look at me and say, "boy you better stop playing if you know whats good for you!" Then to show me what you are talking about, you drop it low and pick it up real slow. And as you pick it up back to standard height, I make my way over to you, and catch you bending you over to touch your toes. With your sweetness all exposed, I sneak up behind you and plant my tongue against your lower lips.

Nibbling and playing your clit and playing with it between the gap in my front teeth, I grip your ass as I pull you closer and nearer.

I began licking up and down, round and round, sticking my tongue deep into your body til your moans are evident. As your body starts to shake, I move my tongue upward to tickle your glory hole. The mere touch of my tongue against it as it circles it, you begin to shutter and quiver.

Holding this position I pull away and lightly blow around the wet spot I created and watch you wiggle, making sure I get all of it air dried.

Lowering my face again back to blow, lick and suck in between your thighs, I now got all type of your juices just dripping on my face. Smashing your bottom in my face I can only defend myself by licking and licking those lips with an occasional stiff tongue jammed up in you.

As you release me and I am free. I fall back on the floor and just lay there as you capture your opportunity; you move toward my feet stopping with tender pussy juices just dripping all over my dick. As I grab my dick and hold it steady, you lower yourself down and onto it til my entire dick is swallowed by you and all the goodness.

Just sitting there with me all in, you start to move nice and slow, winding up. As you start to ride my dick with your back facing me, I feel an uncontrollable urge to give you a slap on the ass as you are riding and riding. I slap your ass and watch it jiggle, ohh I love that nice big ass!!!

With every move you make, I throw a nice hump at the end of it. That hump sends shock waves trickling down your back; riding your spine all the way down. Feeling every inch of my dick hitting your walls, I grab your waist and pull you down as I pump up. With an arch in my back, I start pumping faster, and faster. Feeling me speed up, you change positions and now is facing me, with your legs planted and a crouching stance, you drop your ass in a way that I wasn't ready for.

Up and down, up and down, bobbing right on the head is sending new signals to my brain. As I try to fight that feeling, my grip on your waist gets tighter as I try to hold you down as I start to un-load my entire load within your sweet box of love.

As my body fills your body up, you never stop, still moving to your own rhythm, with each move up I can see my syrup trying to escape from your body. A look that cannot be duplicated unless done in the same manner it was given in. Without knowing what is going on I start cumming again!

As my subsequent load squirts at a pressure that you can feel hitting your walls, you throw your head back and start to ride aggressively as you are starting to cum with me. Coming together, your place your hands on my waist and start to ride like you are trying to tame me. Your hip movements get more forceful as you swing them right, left, forward and backward. The way you are riding is like watching you with the hula-hoop and you are the champion!!! Then you do something new, you turn your body to the left and lean that way a lil bit as you start just twerk that ass in real quick motions. With them fast motions right on the tip of my dick you got me moaning to that sexual god!!

That did it!

Just as my body start to shot, you jump off and grab my dick and point it straight up in the air and just watch my charge shoot up 2feet in the air and land on my stomach.

oh what a feeling, as we finish and you wipe up my liquid mess, you position your legs right alongside of mine and lay on me completely. Feeling refreshed, I wrap you up in my arms and we just lay there on the floor til we both fall asleep.

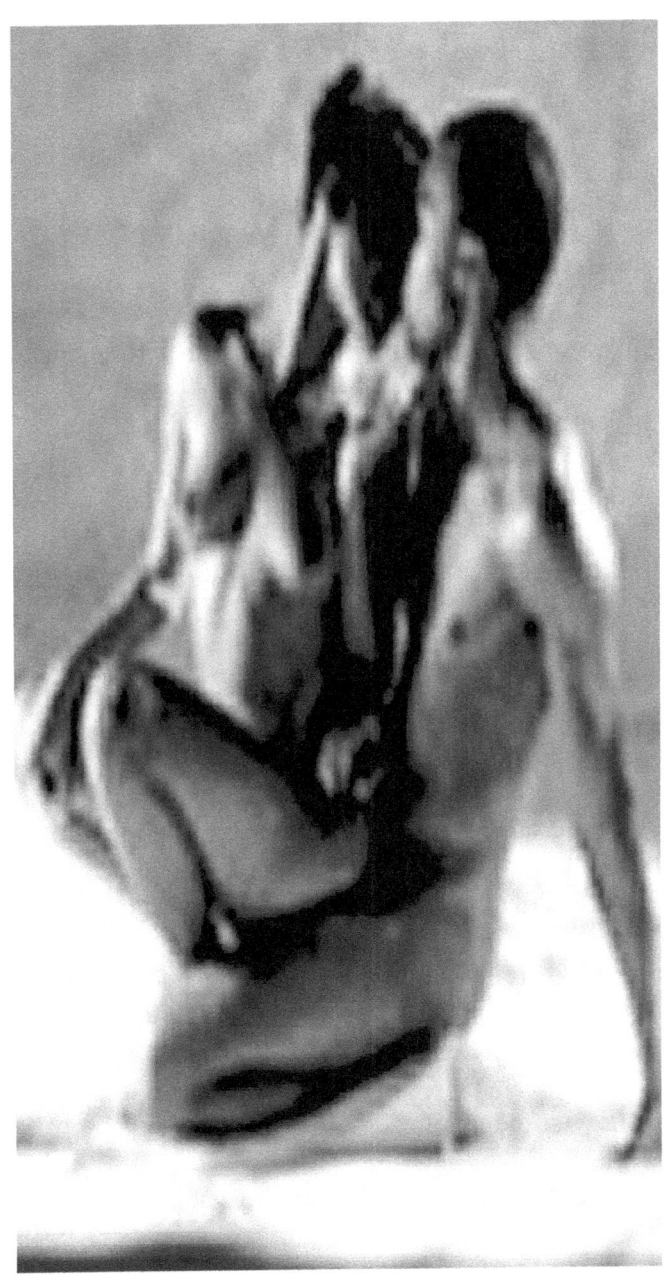

Just A Kiss

The first date, he takes you to a nice restaurant
something real nice that made you feel like a queen.
Then from there the both of you took a walk along
the waterfront in Battery Park. Feeling liked you
must of walked and walked as you talked and talked
for hours. To end your first date, you find
yourselves at a quaint little spa that you don't even
remember how you got there.

Once there, he had the staff start preparing you for
what he called the 'Seductive Bliss' package. The lil
petite lady took you to a private room and handed
you a pile of items to put on. Un-robing yourself
from your own clothes, without hesitation you put
on every item they had laid on the bench; a pair of

cloth like bikinis with bra and a super, fluffy, oversized white robe. Once you were completely ready you came from the room to be greeted by that same staff member. Taking you to the juice bar and fixing you a health drink, it was nice and sweet and you couldn't help but ask for more, (that was the fat girl in you).

After he took care of everything at the front desk, he later joined you at the juice bar. He too was wearing a super fluffy oversized robe; you know he got on only a pair of cloth like underwear, "hahaha"

Asking if your drink is good, he orders the same thing. As you sat there his voice was like your favorite record; his eyes had me staring at him with that deer in the headlights look. You were totally captivated by this man and his impression of a first date.

Grabbing you by your hand he tells you he wants to give you a tour. Getting up from your seats, you start your special tour. The first stop, he showed you the herbal mist steam room, (even though you were very interested you knew not to go in with your hair). Onto the hot rocks sauna formed like an igloo, (just touching the door you can feel how hot it must be in there), leaving there he took you to an interesting array of tubs; the 3 dipping pools. He explained that one was for cleaning with the lemon, the other is for stimulating your skin with ginger, and the last is to pamper your skin with rose petals).The tour ended with the water scrub tables and to the private massage rooms. Smiling from ear to ear you are just floored that you are here and able to experience this for once in your life.

Just as he was finishing his tour duties, a staff member comes over and whispers into his ear. He then leads you to an elevator where it takes us up one more floor to a dimly lit hallway. Now in this dimly lit hallway you can barely hear the sound of water moving about.

Getting to where that water sound is coming from; as you walk through the door you are awed by what you see!! Candles were everywhere there must have been over a hundred of them. A huge tub which looked as if it could fit 4 people with spare room, this tub is filled with water and on top of the water are rose petals (lots of them!). In the corner is a bottle of something in an ice bucket with long stem glasses next to it. On the other side of the glasses is a plate of cut up fruit.

As he helps you take off your robe, you get goose bumps up and down your arms, goose bumps from the thought of being pampered like this.

As you get into the water you feel the troubles of the world dissolving away; you now understand the old school "CALGON" commercial.

Lowering your body into the water completely, you see him taking off his robe and letting it hit the floor. As he steps into the water you get all excited from the thought of him being so close and so near to you. In the water, he reaches over and grabs the glasses of poured champagne.

Sitting on one side of the tub, he moves close to you with a glass extended. Taking a sip, you can feel the feel the bubbles hitting the back of your throat.

Taking in all the sights, sounds, and experience you are feeling, you find yourself comfortable and relaxed. Feeling very good and receptive to his touch in every way! You get to touching and caressing each other in a very sensual way of affection. It is just something with the way his hands touch your neck; the way his hands touch your thighs.

You loved the way the water got his skin glistening and looking so juicy! Not being able to help yourself, you lean into him and kiss on his neck and shoulders. It is like an aphrodisiac is in the air. you can't seem to stop touching this man!

Without getting intimate, you touch and kiss each other's bodies like crazy. Laying your head back as he hoovers over you, he removes your bra and licks from behind your right ear down your neck then down the front of your chest till he is on your breast with great sucking motions,." Oh my, what am I going to do?"

About an hour into this session, he got your blood pressure up and circulating into every inch of your body. What are you going to do with this man?!?!!Just as you can feel your weakness taking over there is a knock on the door; it is one of the staff telling you that you have only 15minutes left before the end of our private 'Seductive Bliss' package.

Getting yourselves up and out of the water, he dried

your body from head to toe. With each pat he

massaged your muscles with such care that you

could of swore some moisture just leaked out of

your body. After he got you dressed in what you

came in, he quickly threw on his robe and led you

out of the room. Back down stairs you both got

dressed and met up at the front reception desk.

After tipping the staff we left the spa. As you

walked out in the fresh night air, you didn't know

what to do with yourself. You thought you wiped up

all your juices as more came out, but you guess not

as your panties are now damp.

Getting back home with a huge smile on your face.

This man, who was the most perfect gentleman this

whole evening, leans in to kiss you good night. As his lips touch yours you feel a spark. For a kiss that seemed like it was going on for more than an hour. Pressed up against his body, feeling his warmth, feeling his hands as they hold you tight my body just melts into his touch.

As you walk through the door you start to think about the whole night, out of everything that happened this night, the only thing that is more on your mind than anything else is, the goodnight kiss, that good night kiss from your prince charming.

Parking Lot

After a night on the town starting off with dinner at
the Statler Grill serving us some Colorado Lollipop
Lamb Chops for appetizers; followed by a nice
Porter House Steak for me and a plate of Alaskan
Salmon for you, we had a full night ahead of us.
After dinner we went to Caroline's Comedy Club
for the 1030pm show of Paul Mooney, who had you
in stitches all night long. Then not to end the night,
we went to see the Punany Poets. Their way with
words had you in the mood, I felt like I should have
tipped them for helping on this first date.

During the show I saw you touching yourself and
you were getting intense with every poem as it was
recited. Sensing my chance, I put my hand on yours

as it nestled deep in-between those thighs. By the time the show was over, my right hand was buried under your skirt and touching way past them lace panties.

As we leave the theater we decide to go and get a bite to eat so as I start up the truck, my mind is set on going to a local diner in my area about 20 minutes away.

Now as I am driving down the Westside Highway heading to the Holland Tunnel, I feel your hands as they cross the border into the country of "My Pants". Trying to improve relations you unzip them, reach in and come up with something to your likening. Still focusing on the road, I almost lose my damn mind as your lips hit the head. The warmth of your lips feels so good I had to remember I was doing 65 down the Westside Highway!! As you lower your head down to completely hide my dick within your mouth I can feel myself drifting off again into bliss as the truck swerves a lil. Stroking my dick and looking up at me you say, "You hold this thing steady and I'll hold this dick steady deal?" And just as I was about to say deal, you take him into your mouth again and do some things with your tongue and cheek.

Passing by Chelsea Piers now, my thought was to pull over and gets it truly popping up in here! But pressing the gas down speeding past it, I am just along for the ride. Tugging on him with your lips, I can feel myself letting go of that built up pressure. Coasting through the Holland Tunnel, I explode all up in your throat. Not stopping now, you continue to lick, kiss and suck all of it out of me with such zeal.

Thinking ok, we are back into Jersey City, and wow! What a nut!!!!

But that isn't the end....

Sitting up with your left hand still stroking him, you look at me as you lick your lips, asking me if I got any more for you. Smiling from ear to ear, I nod my head to signal yes I do.

Pulling up in the parking lot of the diner and backing the truck in nice and snug between two other trucks, I get out and start to fix my pants and shirt. Just then you get out and call out to me to come to the back of the truck to help you.

Getting to the back I grab your waist and ask what can I help you with? Grabbing my hand you pull up your skirt and place my hand near your wet dripping pussy. I realize you have on no panties. Before I could unzip my pants you were already there pulling me out of them pants once again.

Turning around I grab hold of your waist with my left hand as I push into you with my right hand, guiding my hard dick in to your sanctuary. With all the moisture you already have, I glide on in nice and smoothly.

As you feel me entering, you back up a lil, then start to move in a rhythm of "in and out". With only half of him in, your body starts to shake; your body starts to quiver. Grabbing your hair I pull hard making you come back more onto my stiff and fully erect dick. Lowering my stance just enough so that I am angled so that with each thrust I go up and in deeper and stronger. Throwing this dick up in you til I feel what feels like I am hitting the back wall touching your spine, I continue this throwing of a pelvic swirl into the mix, left to right to left I bend making sure you feel all of me in you.

Feeling stuffed, your moans are getting louder, not wanting to get caught in a diner parking lot, I let your hair go and grab your neck. Pulling your neck til your head is turned up toward your left shoulder and back I got total control!

Pulling out of you, I can see your juices all over my dick, and I am not talking about that clear juice, you let out that good white juice!

Taking my dick and beating your bare exposed ass with it you start to move back to feel the hardness of it. So just as you are trying to back up onto it, I stuff it in you once more!

"Is this what you want?!?!?"

A nice slap of your ass with my left hand you respond loud and clear, "yes daddy!!!"

Riding now you brace yourself by putting up your hands against the truck, but the bucking we doing got you re-adjusting your hands before you fall and hit your face.

Just as we getting it in with no stopping, a car pulls up into the parking lot, so not to be caught we shift to another spot behind the truck. As the car is gone and out of our sight, we continue to where we left off like nothing interrupted us at all.

With both hands on your hips, I pull and throw you on this dick like you never felt before! As my actions get more intense and deliberate, I feel your body about to give way and release some more of your good flow.

Feeling it about to come out, you tell me what you are about to do and want to know if I could join you? Not trying to let you have all the fun, I whisper loud enough for you to hear me, "yes, baby I am cumming too!!!!"

As we both explode and our juices mix together within you, and as I pull out, you feel it seeping as I can actually see it leaking out. Grabbing a t-shirt from the back of the truck, I hand it to you to catch it all before it stains your skirt and/or shoes.

Cleaning up, we head on into the diner to get a bite to eat.

After spending about an hour and a half eating and talking, we pay the bill and leave out back to the truck.

As we drive off you again place your hand in my lap and casually rub my dick. Trying not to break any laws, but wanting to get home in a hurry, we pull up at my front door.

Parking and getting through the doors, we are now in the living room, with you bent over the sectional couch looking out the window.

With me deep within your sugar walls, I lift up your butt and separate them cheeks to make sure I am all up in there! Driving each stroke home, driving each pump straight to the point of relaxing and riding the wave, your body just releasing all of its sweet sticky juices.

Playing with your pussy by pushing in deep and pulling out quick only to do it again and again. Seeing more and more of your silky juice coating me is turning me on more and more! Throwing my dick way up in you, you turn back to look and make sure it is still me back there driving you wild.

Spreading your legs and lifting them up I am pulling your legs back to make sure you are getting this entire dick! While stuffing my dick in you in a push and pull motion we hear your pussy talking up a storm.

Not knowing what to do cause you never had your pussy fart so loud before, you just say fuck it!

Getting it in while in this awkward position and the hearing your pussy talk back like that has you truly going crazy! Your body is not under your control at all; all of a sudden you feel it and can't stop it.

Pumping hard and long with the push and pull of your legs I can feel your body shaking. Thinking it is just a regular cum, like 5minutes ago, I pay it no mind, and I get in to my rhythm something seriously! Your built up pressure pushed me back and out of you. Now your body is releasing in such force, you squirt all over me as it drips down your and my legs.

Letting your legs go as they are shaking too much, you just lay there over the couch back and I stumble and end up leaning against a wall.

As the rest of my cum just drips down my leg I pay it no attention as I am drained of all my energy and wondering how can I still be standing.

Making my way to the couch, I just lay on the cushion under where you are still laying over the couch back.

Mustering up all the energy you got left in your body; you grab my dick and stroke it as I fall to asleep.

PlayTime

Using your GPS and still getting lost.

Getting to his house a lil late, but still looking classy in your jeans and sweater top covered by your fitting jacket. You kiss him as he opens the door. There I stand with my big broad shoulders being covered in that milk white T-shirt hugging my upper frame oh so well and my sweat pants loose but with tension just right to see them strong thoroughbred thighs I got. Looking me up and down, you know exactly why you broke your neck to come see me as soon as you got back in town from LA. Walking past me you try your hardest to play it cool, but my scent just took you by the arm, scooped you up and body slammed you with lustful sensations! You can honestly admit it now, you have never wanted another man as much as you want, no you need me!

You enter my loft under my direction, so I take you to the living room and ask you to get comfortable as possible. Removing your jacket and scarf, you sit on the sectional part facing the kitchen under the upstairs section which you can only imagine to be a bedroom area. Looking around you can see that I keep things nice, neat and organized. The couch is wonderful firm brown leather with accented orange pillows; the pictures hanging on the walls are all done in a black and white renaissance theme, very interesting and inviting. The hard wood floors glisten like water as the huge floor to ceilings windows let in just the right amount of light.

Thinking to yourself, this is very nice, a chick can get use to being here.

Sitting next to you, I inform you that dinner will be ready in about 15minutes. Second thing through your mind is, "he can cook to?!?!?" Oh you are loving this so far.

Standing up as if to show you how I look in sweatpants and a T-shirt I ask you what you wanted to drink. You reply some wine would be great, and I disappear into the kitchen only to reappear with 2 glasses and a bottle of Moscato. Sipping on your glass as you look into my eyes, listening to me tell you what I am cooking for you is like a special serenade to your ears. On the menu is jumbo prawns, pan fried with a touch of garlic, parsley and a dash of lemon juice with an asparagus risotto.

Your mouth is watering just thinking of the flavors I

mentioned so passionately.

Now the conversation takes a turn, a turn you didn't

even see coming. I ask about you, your day, your

hobbies and how you spend your past time. Listen,

you are not afraid to talk about yourself but me

being interested in you just threw you off guard.

Helping you up by giving you my hand, we head to

the dining room where I sit you down so I can go

and get the dinner on plates. Better than you had

imagined, the plate presentation was of a 5 star

restaurant and just like a well satisfied food critic,

you gave my cooking nothing but high marks.

Feeling too good from the meal you just ate, you

really didn't want to move. So we actually just sat at

the table and talked a lil more. The conversation

touched on so many topics within about an hour and a half time frame which left you truly amazed. The topics ranged from books just read, to current events, to the days when you were a lil girl and I was a lil boy to what we both wanted out of life.

I grab your hand and coyly lean over and whisper in your ear, it is time for dessert. Your mind went somewhere else for a moment, "oh my god!!!".

I get up and within 5 minutes I come back with one plate with tiramisu and some ice cream. The tiramisu was so damn good you had to test me and ask, "where did you buy that from?" Quick on my feet I respond, "All the ingredients from the supermarket down the street."

Getting up from the table we go to a room off the living room, on the door it says "Play Time". In this room is a pool table, some comfortable looking chairs, a huge flat screen TV mounted to the wall and a black piano lacquer pool table with a red felt top. Pointing to the table I ask you if you play. Feeling good from the wine and pampering, you get a lil sassy, "I will beat your ass up in here!!!"

Hearing the challenge, I accept while upping the ante, "wow really?!?!? Then let's play a game of strip pool? Every ball you knock in, I have to take off an item, for every 2 balls I make you have to take off an item til one of us is totally naked."

Thinking to yourself, "I can't be that bad at pool." Then saying it loud enough for me to hear you

clearly say back with, "ok you are on, let's go you
rack'em!!"

After breaking and not making any ball into a
pocket, you look toward me as it is my go. Now
trying to give you a fighting chance, I miss a
perfectly good shot on purpose. Feeling yourself,
you take your shot making in 2 balls (the 4 and the
11). Looking at me you say, "yeah buddy, take off 2
items!!! Do I get to pick what comes off?"

As I take off my t-shirt to reveal a tank top
underneath, I shake my head no to your question
and proceed to remove my tank top. Now my chest
muscles are fully visible and tempting you, so to
fight your inner temptation, you bite your lip.
Standing in front of you, I motion for you to go

again to which you are so distracted that you miss the next shot. Oh no, it is my turn now.

Thinking to yourself you got on at least 9 items before you are completely butt naked, you just stand in the corner and smile all the while thinking of making at least 3 more shots to see me butt naked.

I make my first shot by sinking the 6 ball, and then I paused for you to remove an item. After you remove all your jewelry thinking it was a safe move, I knocked in 6 more balls (1, 5, 14, 3, 2, and the 7). Now you are down to only 3 items left; your bra, panties and socks. How did you get here like this, you start to think damn!!! "It is still his turn to shoot?" , the only thing going through your mind now is, and "will I get to see him remove his clothes before I have to?" You guess not, I make 3 balls

(15, 12, and 9) needed to win this game. With you standing there fully exposed with no type of cover at all, to redeem yourself, you make a special wager with me, "if you knock in the rest of the balls I will be your slave for the next hour". Something should of told you that you were going to lose when I quickly replied, "bet!!". I proceeded to knock in the remaining balls 10, 13, 8 and the 14.

With you butt naked and willing to honor our bet, you open your arms to me as if saying, "I am yours"

Placing balls back on the table I stop to think about my first command for the hour. Putting my pool stick on the table and taking yours from you, I then issue my first official command by whispering in your ear, "sit up here on the table, and lay your head back."

Helping you on the table by practically getting deep

in-between your thighs, the next thing you know

you are laying back gracing my pool table, reaching

back knocking balls around. Still in between them

thighs, I lower myself down to a height just perfect

to look directly into your eye of love.

Opening your legs by parting your thighs, I move in

closer, and then without a warning at all, I poke you

in your eye of love with my tongue. That feeling

right there, that feeling right motherfuckin there!!!

You let out the most beautiful sounded moan of

relief I have ever heard!

With the tip of my tongue moving like a pen on

paper, you can feel the beautiful words Iam saying

to your moistened pussy. All the adverbs,

metaphors, pronouns and adjectives in every sentence and every punctuation.

Grabbing and holding on to pool balls to keep from exploding; your eyes continue to roll to the back of your head as if a sexual poltergeist has taken over your body! Getting in deeper with my licks, you can feel the warmth of my face near your inner thigh, you feel my chin as it is nestled in that spot just below your pussy but right above your ass hole. As I am sucking and teasing your clit with precision lips, tongue and mouth movement, I feel your body letting some juices escape. My hands are wrapped around your lower body in such a way that your right leg is on my left shoulder while your left leg is pinned under my right arm. In this position your sweetness is exposed and truly out in the open.

Rising up, I take my right hand and start to slap that wet dripping, throbbing and swollen pussy. With each slap your body responds with micro shutters and on that last slap, you squirt, just enough to let me know I am once again needed for some one on one attention. As if I never left her and your pussy jump right back into a good good conversation, a long good licking conversation.

As I feel your body about to bust, I grip you just right and pull you in nice and tight, as I start with a pattern of licking that does it for you, got you calling out my name in the same sentence with "oh my god!". This pattern is nothing new, but I perform it oh so special, the way I circle your clit with the tip of my tongue, and then I use the fat part of my tongue to rub against your overly sensitive clit! The way I lick down the side of your vagina and lick in a full circle til I am back where I started. The way I dig my tongue into you, and move my tongue around your hole with a slight amount of pressure. The way I have my hands with your legs up and controlling you by rolling you back and forth with each lick. The way I lick and flick my tongue at the sweet spot under your pussy, like it is a button of sensuality. The way I roll you back and just happen to let my tongue explore your ass.

Your body is so responsive that you lose control, your leg muscle tighten up on you, your thighs start to twitch, your arms shake feverishly as I am doing the damn thing!!!

Focusing my attention on your clit, you can feel my left arm changing position, not knowing what else to expect, I go and do it to you, I stick my finger into you at the same time I is tantalizing your clit! You have no choice like you are suddenly hit with a case of Tourette, "What are you trying to do to me!?!?!?"

As if I knew your body for years and years, I got it talking to me in languages you would have only imagined! Oh! Oh! Ooooohhhhhh! I got you to squirt with enough pressure to whistle. You unload all of your natural juices in a steady stream like flow. You swear you wet up my nice looking pool table, but at this point, you know I didn't give a fuck!!! The only thing on your mind is my mother fucking tongue! Damn, if they sold that in stores, you would be a clepto-maniac for real!!

"Oh My God, I am still cumming, how do you shut this off; I can't be cumming like this".

In the back of your head, "This man is something else; he is still touching all the right buttons, licking all the right keys, sucking on all the right points……"

As you lay there on my pool table completely drained and relaxed at the same damn time, you truly don't know what to do with yourself. I get up; wipe my mouth and just smile, smiling like I knew I just laid it down on you. How dare me, how dare me know that you can't even sit up right now, and you can only imagine trying to walk would be like a baby horse trying to walk for the first time.

Helping you up, I get you dressed, walked you to your car, gave you a kiss good morning and called you to make sure you got home safe and sound. As you went to take off your jacket and put it on a hanger, there was something in your right pocket, I wrote a note that said, "If you feel up to it, be at my house at the same time tomorrow night."

Let's just say, you will be there tomorrow, you won't be wearing that many items of clothing, and damn it you won't be late at all!!!!!!!!!!!!!!!

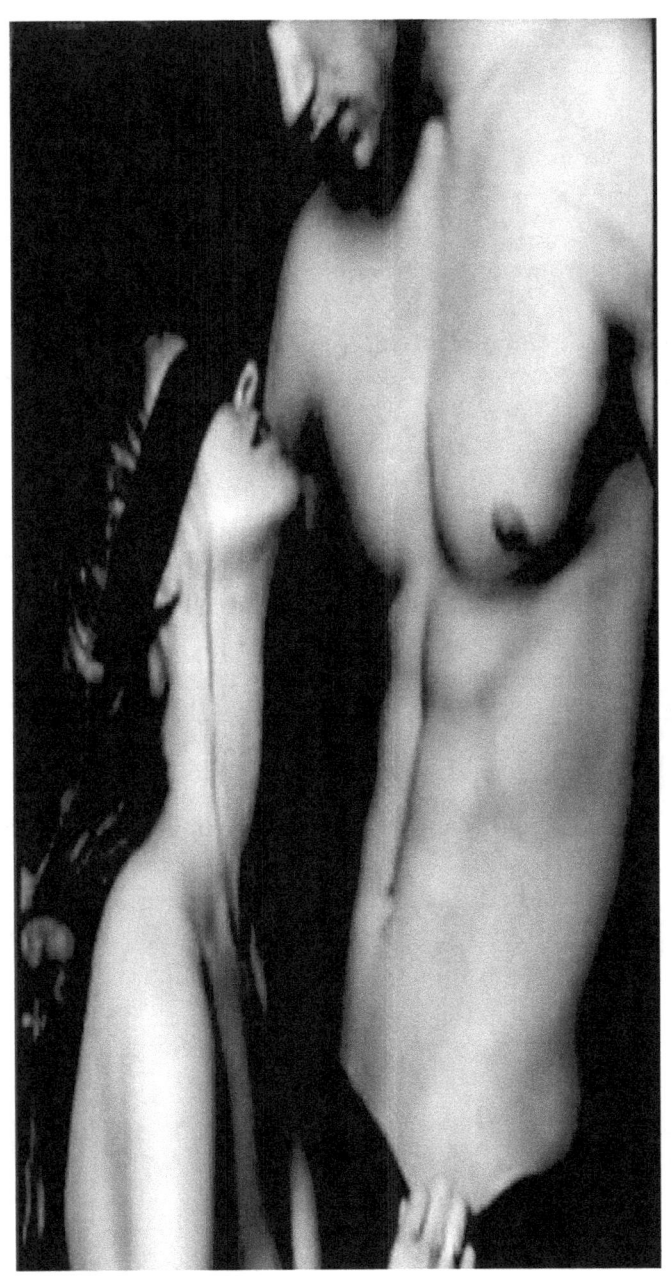

Pleasure

Sitting here in a foreign city about 586.45 miles away from you and my mind is flooded with pure sensual thoughts of you. Laying down in that big lonely king bed for a lonely man.

Going through my phone looking at the special pictures you sent me about an hour ago, the lights are off and the only thing lighting up the room is the laptop playing old school love songs. The photo album has 10 awesome pictures of you and that wonderful body. Is it getting hot in here or is it just me? Removing all clothing to be completely free I now feel my hands touching my inner thigh.

Looking at the pictures I can feel an excitement growing fast and moving upward. Closing my eyes,

I can see it very clear "live and in color". You walk up to the bed and reach out to push my hand away from touching myself only to put your hands where mine once was. Stroking my dick with your right hand you feel the pressure building up, that one vein under the dick getting full and fat and the head swells up to penetration size. With your left hand you gently caress my balls is a very seductive way.

Leaning over you take your tongue and circle the head with it. Squeezing the shaft, you cover the head with your lips and I let out a pleasingly sigh of relief. Teasing the head while stroking with a tight grip around the shaft you still massage and play with my balls. Opening up my legs, you climb on the bed to get in between them. Now you are directly in front of that good good and you show your appreciation to that by moving my dick to the left side as you lick and kiss my balls.

Still stroking you continue to kiss, suck and lick me in such a way that shocks and awe me. With your tongue you trace a path up to the head tip.

Dropping the mouth over the top and engulfing me in your mouth feels so good!! Repeating this several more times you move your hand from my balls to help withhold my dick as you do what you are there to do. Trying to take me all in your mouth you feel good cause going all the way down you left 2 inches untouched, but your saliva drips down to the base.

With each up and down movement you start to get yourself excited more and more. Your grip starts to get more defined and your movements start to get more in sync. The tricks you are doing now got me feeling real good!!!

Going all the way down and coming back up with your teeth lightly touching the head; going down one side and coming up on another side, and the way you swirl and circle your tongue around the head with quick sucks in 3 to 5 pumps.

Moving your hands up to grip and squeeze my chest as you look up at me while performing your beautiful tricks I can feel that pipe getting filled with that good warm silky smooth jizm. That feeling has my legs stiff and a hump in my back; feeling my body movement you don't stop, you know what is happening and you continue to press, I mean suck on.

As my body excitement climbs and climbs you start

to speed up your rhythm. Grabbing my dick and pumping with every suck you give, twisting with every lick you give, and then it happens.

As the arch in my back get intense, my eyes are rolled to the back of my head you read my thoughts, you grab me with both hands and start to suck the nectar from its root! As each squirt comes forth you are there to meet it with nothing less than suck, lick and spit.

Just as the last drop of what seems like a gallon of syrup hits my thigh and runs down, I open my eyes to the reality of an empty hotel suite where I am all alone in this huge king bed.

I pick up the phone and dial your number, sleepily you answer and all I say is "thank you that was great!" I hang up before you can even question me I

fall right to sleep.

Home Alone

Packing up the kids to spend the night with their godparents, you have only one thing on your mind, some good good!

As you travel across town to drop off the kids, Ray gets to your house and starts his set up.

When you walk through the door you find Ray (dressed in a white t-shirt, dark denim jeans with those nice brown shoes you loved in the store window) waiting on you with the lights dim, a glass in his hand and music playing in the background. Making your way to him your face just shows the relief you are anxious to experience. Taking his glass you take a quick sip then with no regard just throw it to the side with a loud crash.

Jumping into his arms he grabs you with such passion that you feel your body release a lil right there and then. Putting his hands on each side of your face you and him engage in a kiss that makes movies! With your free hands you caress and explore his terrain like body; from the ridges in his stomach to the hills of his chest to the pipeline veins running through his granite formed arms.

The next thing you know you are pulling off his shirt! Like magic his upper body is instantaneously exposed. Now rubbing his bare skin your hands begin to shake at the opportunities to do what you want, how you want with no fear of the kids interrupting. Kissing down his neck, then to his left breast, then nibbling on his right nipple, making your way to is stomach as your hands massage his breast you can't wait any more. You feel him

pulling you up, as you rise he turns you around and

presses his body into yours, giving you a feelings of

his rock hard tree trunk lying beneath them nice

fitting jeans. In this position he proceeds to

unbutton your pants and ever so gently remove

them from your body. Next he frees your body from

that blouse that hid everything it this long, grabbing

your hands, he leads you to the bedroom where he

then sits you down and helps them pretty round

breast breathe by getting rid of that constraining

bra. As you move on the bed into position at the

edge of the bed, he stands there as you help him out

his jeans. The only problem is, you couldn't focus

when you saw his bulge coming through his boxer

briefs. You just had to touch it, hell you wanted to

suck and kiss it right away! With him helping you focus you finish removing his jeans.

Then like an episode of 'snapped' you lose it, you rip his underwear from his body and grab what you waited for all day! With both hands around it, it is now inserted into your hot mouth where you playfully lick, kiss, suck and tickle it like it is the best thing going. With your right hand you caress and knead his balls while still enjoying yourself of every inch of him. Feeling him get even harder you grab his cheeks with both hands as you pull him in closer taking all of him in your mouth. Reaching your limit, you push him away as you start to gag!

Regaining your composure, you quickly put him back in your mouth. Feeling up and down his thighs you also feel a lil wetness escape your body.

His hands come out of nowhere and grip your head as he starts pumping, as he starts gyrating even more, as he starts to fuck your mouth with pure power. His body reaches his peak and climax you brace yourself for his load to shoot out.

As he unloads his warm silky syrup you don't let up, you feel its warmth as it slides back and coats your mouth as it makes its way down your throat with a series of gulps.

Making sure you got every last drop you continue to suck and lick til you notice his knees buckle. Rising up you wipe your face with your right arm and lay back on the bed and a very seductive pose.

Like a pack of wild pit bulls unleashed on a paper bag of meat he jumps on the bed and just rips them panties right off of you. You might even have a lil nick on your thigh from it.

Spreading your legs he puts on display his menu for the night! Them luscious thighs with a glisten from your early pre-cum wetness, your supple breast with them nipples just looking for some attention! Starting at your left ankle, kissing and licking it with nothing but sheer lust, he works his way up to the back of your knee cap. He moves up slowly to make sure to taste every inch of your body, as he glides over your juicy wet pussy, he lets out a huge moan! But like a man on a mission he continues up and across your mid section, gripping your right breast in his hand with enough force to change its form. He teases your left nipple. With every flick of his tongue, you arch your back with an unbelievable sensation. Grabbing the sheets and balling them up in your hands you can't help but to let him know you like what he is doing!

Reaching his left hand up to touch your face, your grab it and put his pointer finger in your mouth, as you suck on his finger, he starts to entice your right breast. Kissing and nibbling on your areola he can feel your other hand on his back, rubbing his back and pulling him into you, with each pull you feel his kisses get even more pronounced!

Oh that feeling!!!

As he makes his way back down the right side of your body he kisses, nibbles, licks and sucks on all the same points he touched on the right side of your body. This time when he passed over your throbbing pussy, he can smell that awesome aroma it is putting out to attract him.

Finishing up with your ankle, he moves into close proximity of your nectar. Hovering about it like a bee in flight, he swoops in to kiss it real quickly. Returning to his hovering position, he licks his lips. Lowering himself, he cradles your thighs under them granite formed arm! Holding you in the position with all your goodness on display, he moves in for another taste. Having a nice conversation with your clit, he pulls away to suck on that part of your inner thigh where that big tendon is. With his tongue he moves to the other side tracing his path.

Your hands are now shaking at the long awaited and anxious release you want so bad!

Tracing his path again, he stops and digs his tongue deep into you. Feeling around with just his tongue, you can feel every taste bud on his tongue as it slides over you. As he licks up from that wet moist opening to the top of your perky clitoris, he takes your clit into his mouth and sucks on it while circling it with his tongue.

Pulling your legs closer into his body, he takes your clit between his 2 front teeth and teases it with all his might. With his head turning sideways you know he is really putting in work!

Releasing your clit, he licks just around the hood of your clit then without warning he drops down low and licks vigorously just below your dripping wet pussy. Your moans are louder now then you would of ever guessed. Licking back up, his lips are one on one with your lower lips. I proceed to tongue kiss to where you feel it bubbling up inside of you.

He notices you got more sweet juices running down between them thighs. Just before your sweetness disappears he rotates your body up and lets his tongue get all of it. Just as he is rolling your body, his tongue hits you right in-between them pretty cheeks. Just then, just at that very second, you let out more than a sexual moan; your body let out a call of the wild! Your thighs shake, your hands tremble to where you can't control them at all, and your voice is high pitched as you call out to GOD for help!

As he continues to lick you in that special spot, your body shoots out some of that warm sticky flow. Feeling your cum hit him, he just continues to lick, and lick! After 5 more licks, you are tapping out like a wrestler on TV. Easing up he returns to your squirting pussy, as he licks and sucks up what came out already. He hits that button again and she lets loose with more juices. This time with his mouth right there he is on the job.

Clenching your eyes tight from the ecstasy you reach your hands down and grab his head. As you pull his face in harder and harder you cum more and more til it is like a pipe with too much back pressure!

Backing his face away from that pipe, he climbs up on top of you with his dick in his right hand. He pushes the head right up against your lips as you throw your head back in anticipation of what is to come next. He moves in lil by lil. Your facial expression with you biting your lip and eyes rolled to the top of your head say it all!

With him fully inside of you, he pauses to give you a chance to let it out. Grabbing you by placing his arms underneath you and holding onto your shoulders he starts to thrust up and forward while kissing your exposed neck. In total sync as each kiss touches you, you can feel him deep within you. With your arms wrapped up around him, you sigh, moan and ohh as you continue to ride that pleasure. That ride that is taking you through several time zones, several hemispheres, all while still laying on your back in your own bed.

Switching positions to where you are now on your right side and he is sitting up, he penetrates you with ease! As he slides in, your body shutters and releases more juices to coat him. Placing his left hand on your left thigh, he develops an arch in his back with that perfect angle. Every stroke is hitting that spot with just enough force to make your tender pussy tighten up and try to grab his dick on its own. Swirling his big dick from left to up right to down, he just continues to hit that spot, and as he keeps tapping it he feels your body juices building up.

With his right hand holding down your left arm you reach out and grab his right thigh, digging your nails into him as he drives his dick into you. The sweat is now formed and beginning its descent down his chest, as it falls outside, you notice he has more forming.

Pulling out and back in one rapid movement, you are once again on your back with your legs spread and him acting like you never fed him. Then as quick as he had you in that position he got you in another. Oh My God, you are now straddling him with his dick pointing straight up at your dripping wet, sticky, sweet pussy.

With precise precision, you lower your body slowly onto his. As he watches his dick disappears into the tunnel of bliss, he moans louder. With him half way in, he turns his head and you start to ride. You start off nice and slow then as you get in a steady rhythm you continue to ride it out. Feeling it now, you lower yourself a lil more, but wanting to feel all of it, you lower completely. When he sees you are on your way down, he gives you a quick pelvic pump. The feeling from that is enough to shock and awe you at the same time of pleasing your inner being.

Oh the thin line of pleasure and pain.

Getting your stance right with your feet planted firmly on the bed, your hands gripping his chest. You get to riding as if someone shot a gun in the air or yelled GO!!!!

Well into this position and rhythm your right leg starts to shake. Feeling the situation you try to hold steadfast and ride it out, but just as you thought you had it under control, you release enough fluid to fill a gallon jug. Shaking and releasing you collapse on his chest with him buried deep within you.

Rolling your shaking and squirting body over, he helps get you in position by placing pillow under you to prop you up with your pretty round ass up in the air.

Seeing the perfect opportunity, he enters you in all

his magnificence. As the head moves past the lips,

you sigh, and as he goes deeper, you moan, now

with him in you and pumping his dick you start to

buck back to meet his dick with everything you got.

Looking back to make sure he is the only one back

there he sees you looking. He reaches up and grabs

your neck, squeezing just right, he is choking you

while throwing dick way up in your frame. Feeling

him up in deep to what feels like he is touching

your lung, your moans are loud enough to be heard

by your neighbor!

All of a sudden he uses his hands to grabs your hips

and start driving your ass. With an arch in your

back and an arch in his, he digs deep, long, and

hard!!! Teasing your body by pulling out til the

head is the only thing still in, he grabs the shaft and circles the dick within your walls. That feeling is something else, it drives you crazy. Throwing it back in you he notices some of your sweetness dripping out.

Wanting more and all of him, you back up into him just to get what you want. Feeling the urge trying to take over him, he switches up his rhythm. Pushing you away, he places his tongue where his dick once was. Licking and sucking has you feeling like he is trying to turn you out!

As your body is close to its grand explosion, you beg him for put his dick back inside, inside again so you can cum all over his dick!!!!

That was all that was needed as he tighten his grip on your hips, and starts to pump harder. Feeling his passion as it builds up, you throw his pretty round ass back more and more, as his moans get louder and louder you feel something nice and warm flooding your inner cavity. At that particular moment all that flooding has you wanting to open your flood gates too.

In sync your succulent passion fruit explodes and mixes with his to combine and make a happy hour cocktail!!!! As he collapse on top of you and you on top of those wonderful pillows, the both of you just lay there trying to catch your breath.

You both doze off and wake up to a blaring alarm telling you it is now 8:45am the next morning, time to pick up the kids. As you jump up to go and get the kids he kisses you before you vanish out the door.

Coming back with the kids, he is gone and everything is back to normal as if last night had never happened, but you and your swollen coochie know better.

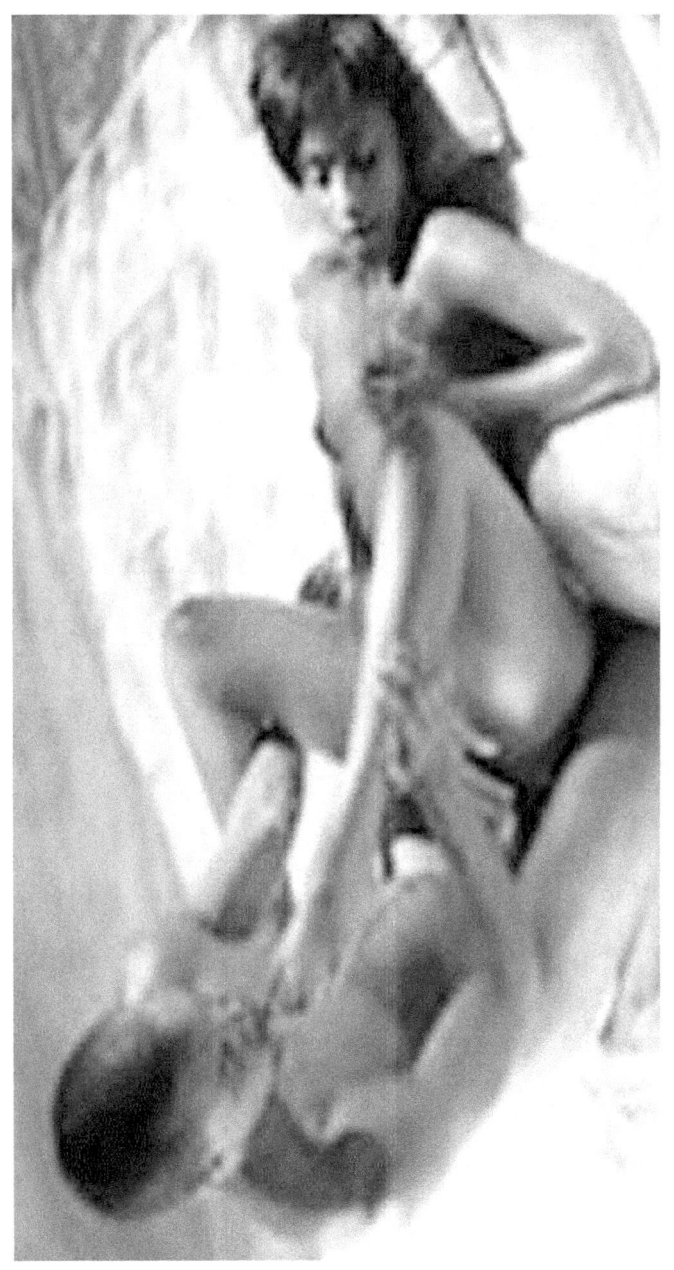

On My Mind At The Time

Hey lady, what about a night of pure unadulterated sex. An evening where as soon as you walk through the door I jump on you and take what I want? Where I bum rush you with kisses and groping while leading you to the bed. Taking off your clothes and just haphazardly throwing them around the room. So incoherent to what is going on, you just now realize that I am completely naked with everything out in the open.

With your back facing the bed, I push backwards and before you can even realize it was the bed, I am on top of you kissing, grabbing and caressing you.

As I move from kissing your soft supple lips down your neck to the side of your right breast, I got both your hands pinned up above your head with my left hand. "Clink Clink", that is the sound of the handcuffs as they are engaged.

Using my left hand I cup and squeeze your breast in a superb preparation for sucking. The right hand has hold of your left thigh cocked up and over my butt in a wrapping position. Still holding onto your breast I start to nibble on your skin on my way down your body. A nibble here, a kiss here, and a lick there, I journey all the way down your right side like it is the New Jersey Turnpike.

Down by your ankles, I got your foot flat on my chest while my hands massage your soles. Kissing my way up but this time I am on the inside lane of this sexual highway coming up to that toll bridge. I nibble right at that very special spot deep within your inner thigh. Using my time just right, I use the thumbs on both hands to spread your moistened lips and hold them in position as I go in and grab your pretty pink clit in mouth. Your body tensed up as your mouth has moans escaping; I know I grab it in the spot now! All of a sudden your hesitating hand try to reach low, but you can't due to the hand cuffs! As your body is under my control, I continue to lick and suck on your clit within ayour hood of lust. With each lick and suck, I turn my head in a different position making sure I got it all in my mouth. Just as I am licking around your swollen clit, your body squirts, your squirting hits me directly on my chin and drains down to create a massive puddle in the middle of the bed! Without a care about the wetness, I play with your clit as if nothing happened.

Moving your right leg up and out, exposing you to me and my lips even more, I lick low and come up making sure I rub your clit with the fat part of my tongue and on the way back down I ensure the tip takes a peek inside you. Pulling back to blow light puffs of air, your body shutters with each puff.

Turn you over onto your stomach with a precision move, I prop you up on the 3 oversized pillows so your your ass is proudly on display. Rubbing some KY Intense on my dick before I insert it into you; holding the shaft, I push the head through them golden doors. As he enters your face changes to an expression of sheer delight. With just the head in I make circular motions with the shaft which in turn makes that huge head in you massage your circular walls. Smacking you on the ass, I tell you, "are you ready for this ride cause I here there is going to be some turbulence?!" To which you moan and yell back, "give it to me you motherfucker! Take this pussy!!! Ooohhhhhh!!!!"

As if on cue, I throw this dick half way in and pull out quickly, only to go in again deeper this time, and pulling out once more. Taking my dick in my hand I slap it against your wet pussy before throwing it back up in all the way. Riding you like you asked, your moans are getting louder. With my left hand I reach under you and start playing with your clit while pushing deep within you.

Breaking up the moans, you scream out, "yes! Yes! Take your pussy!!! You got it right there!!!"

Reaching up with my right hand I grab your neck and pull you back into this dick til my balls are hitting your stomach. So with the left hand playing with your clit, the right pulling you back, balls hitting your stomach and this dick touching your heart, your body releases more sensational milk which now coats every inch of my dick.

Letting me know what I am doing you scream out, "oohhh shit!!!!! Take this pussy, take it!!!!!"

Putting hands on your waist, I get in position to drive this shit home.

Digging deep with push and pull, some left to right motions, some up and downs to put in work. My right hand is gripping your ass with a tight squeeze while my left is pulling and pushing on your waist.

Using my right hand, I pour some warming oil on your bare back while still driving your ass. Spreading that oil on your back you start to feel it warming and then cooling. That changing temperature coupled with the good good sex has you cumming more; having lost count of your body's secretions you just let it all flow.

As your body release, you feel your muscles tighten up and start to cramp in your left thigh. So I change your position to on your back so I can still fuck you and massage that left thigh at the same time. Out of nowhere, your pussy starts to make those farting sounds; like your pussy is speaking to me!

Taking that leg I massage and put it on my shoulder, I drive hard and long, trying to break a bone up in you. Then placing your other leg up on my shoulder, I got you in the 'Huckle-Buck' position! Now I am driving harder and longer trying to move some of your body parts out of the way. With my hands on your waist I forcibly stuff my dick in you with rhythmic pulses and swirling motions. As your body releases more of you, I continue to pump and swirl; as your legs begin to shake I continue to push and pull.

Moving one leg to the same side as the other, now your hole is wrapped around my dick nice and tight. With that much more friction I can feel something rumbling in the lower part of my body. Pulling out to break up the pattern, I beat my dick on your wet pussy. The sound of my dick hitting your wet pussy has that nice ring of "slap slap" and is very very therapeutic to my ears.

Pushing back in you, I turn your legs to the left side and lay them flat while I start back up and thrust my dick in and out of you in passionate movements.

But once inside again, I feel that rumbling feeling starting up again, this time I can feel it moving up my spine. I feel it coursing throughout my veins. Playing with your pussy with just the head in, I develope a huge hump of an arch in my back as I start to groan and moan like a cave man. "Ahhhh. Uuuugggggghhhhhh!!!!!", "take this dick! Oh lord I am cumming!!!"

As my pumps, thrusts, throws and swirls become more definitive, I shoot out with enough built up pressure that you feel it as it hits your inside walls, making your body release your natural juices too. Using your hands to stop my motion, you tell me,

"Baby, please don't move, let me cum all over that dick!!!!".

Staying still as your body ejaculates and mine stream out all the cum I got, I just make small movements to ensure all my cum is gone.

As your muscles relax and your body is spent, I lay down next to you while un-cuffing your wrists. Feeling pleased with what your body just went through; you curl up on top of me with half your body. Your right leg on mine and in between my thighs as your right arm lies on top of my chest and your head resting on my left shoulder.

The next thing I know you are talking gibberish and not making any sense; I just kiss your forehead and tell you to close your eyes and take a nap. While you start to dose off, your right hand reaches down and starts to cuddle my dick. Now I warn you, "wake him up and you will have to put him back to sleep."

Of course not even hearing me, in your sleep you continue to rub and stroke til he starts to wake up. Now with him fully up and hard you still grip him in your sleep. Now as I am laying there with a hard dick wondering what I am going to do with this thing; as if you are sleep walking, you glide your body face to face with that tool in your right hand. Opening your mouth, you put him in and start to suck on it with such tender lips. As your sucking and stroking, my pelvic muscles start to twitch and move in sync with your mouth and hand gestures. With your body positioned with your ass accessible,

I use my right hand to massage and caress you as your sucking gets intense and soothing. My pelvic thrusts become more frequent and deliberate. Loving this feeling I can't help but to cover my forehead with my left hand, the pure pleasure is sending shock waves throughout my body.

No more sleeping routine here, you move your body into a better position to "hum" right on top on my head while playing with my balls in such a way that makes me shoot off a lil pre-cum.

Taking me in your mouth all the way, I can feel your tongue slivering around my shaft with your mouth fully engulfed around my dick. I can feel your tongue as it finds and tickles a big vein underneath my dick.

"Oh shit girl, do that again!!"

My gripping of your ass turns into a slap; my left hand grips your head and makes sure I am face fucking you just right. Taking my right hand I move your ass into a more vulnerable position while you are still sucking, licking and kissing my dick from the shaft to the head. In this position I am able to touch your pussy and not even surprised but it is still nice and wet. With my 2 fingers, I dip into the wetness and play in it a bit.

Inserting one finger in you, I can feel your sucking getting harder, getting wetter, getting more pleasing with every suck.

Feeling your body releasing more wetness from me playing with it, I push your ass into position, in between my thighs. With you here, you still continue to suck, lick and kiss, but now you added running your tongue down my shaft on your way to nibble on my balls. Reaching your right arm underneath my left thigh, you pull me in closer as if you can't get enough of my taste.

My moan, ohhs and ahhs are echoing throughout the room, I can no longer contain myself I am ready to explode!

Feeling the pressure building up, you come back up and put me all in your mouth. At the feeling of that warm mouth again, I shoot off a lil bit of cum, just enough to trickle over your tongue. Rising up you lick your lips as you start to kiss my body on your way up and get in a straddling position. Kicking up one leg you lean to the side as you push my dick into your sweetness, and lower your body back down taking all of me into you. Pressing your hands down on my body for leverage, you are able to rise up and drop down with great enough force to truly feel me way up inside of you. After several more of these actions, your arms start to shake and your wetness starts to drip over my inner thigh. Leaking on me feeling like someone is pouring water on me, you cum, and cum hard.

Digging your nails into my skin, feeling your body cum, I now start to feel that rumbling forming in me again. Holding on to your breast trying to fight the feeling, I start to pump back with enough force to make you bounce up and come back down on my dick. With each bounce, I release and release, my thick sticky fluid is now leaking out of you and blowing back up on my stomach. Making a mess of things, we both finish cumming in pure ecstasy and sensuality.

With me still inside of you, you just collapse on top of me and fall straight to sleep.

Mr Right Now

You don't see each other as often as you would like, but when you do, it is nothing less than magical. The sex is amazing! But it goes deeper, the way he touches you, the way he talks to you, he gives you so much attention that you truly feel as if there is no one else in the world!

He is very attentive to your needs when he is with you and that is all that matters to you. Looking at the clock he must be running late, it is already half pass 8pm. Then there is a knock at the door. Could this be your gentleman caller, haha?

Looking through the peep hole, it's him. You couldn't open the door quick enough. He must be wondering what is going on with all that rattling of the door knob and locks.

As this 6'3" man came in you got all hot and bothered, your champion lover is finally here. Taking his jacket, you get a whiff of his cologne, 'Ralph Lauren Black'. You can barely contain myself. You find yourself rubbing on his jacket in such a seductive way that if that jacket was a man, you would have came right then and there. Watching him walk in a lil bit more, looking at them nice fitting jeans you stare at his racing horse thighs and well-formed ass that is connected to his slim and trim waist. Your eyes see right through that button up shirt as if it wasn't even a factor; your line of sight move up his back studying his chiseled back coupled to them massive shoulders and arms.

You think you just came a lil as you come back to your senses.

Putting his jacket on the hook near the door, you walk with him to the couch and sit next to him as he gets himself settled in.

Offering him something to drink, this man jumps up and gets it his self, bringing back 2 glasses and your bottle of wine you had chilling for tonight. Settling back down, he poured the glasses and you sipped of the sweet grape nectar.

As you just sat there enjoying the conversation and the wine; you didn't even notice him turning on the music to a nice low hum of old school slow jams. Then out of nowhere, while relaxing and totally immersed with everything going on about the room, he grabs my left foot and starts to massage and caress it. Thinking to yourself, "Wow I needed that", you just go with the flow. With every muscle in his hand kneading, caressing, and massaging your foot, you can feel all your worries about him fade away. A thought hits your mind... "Oh my god he is now doing the other foot. What did I do to deserve this treatment tonight?"

With your free foot, you go up his shirt and start playing with his nipple. The feeling of his chest is so divine. Using your foot as another hand you cup, squeeze and rub his body with precision.

Tonight just feels so right, he is massaging your feet, your mind, and your soul. What more can you ask for, wait, he is moving up your legs and massaging your thigh now, did he hear you wish for that?

At this point, you couldn't tell what it was; either the wine, the music, the massaging or that damn man, but you stop him before you explode all over the couch. Let's break it down for you like this.... Sweetheart, have you ever had that one night that was just so sensual and sexual with just light touches, where your body was so receptive to him that you literally thought you were in heaven on cloud 9?!?!? That is how you feel, right now!!

Ok, back to what is going on...
As he stood up, you cannot keep your eyes away from the bulge in his pants, it was like a real trouser snake! you swear, you just saw his dick move, does

it sense your lust? "Haha, girl you tripping, get a hold of yourself".

He goes into the bedroom for about, maybe 10 minutes. When he comes back out, he puts out his hand for you; grabbing it he pulls you up and right into his arms, "oh my! I think I just got bit by that snake". Leading you back to the bedroom, you find it looking just as you left it, or so you thought. You embrace in a tight kiss, one that would make movies great!

Like Houdini, your clothes disappeared; you don't even see where he put them you are now butt naked laying back on the bed, with this man hovering over you bare chested and just some boxer briefs on trying hard to contain that motherfucking beast.

Then everything went black from him putting a scarf over your eyes.

Are you ready for this?

You feel his tongue glide up the left side of your body starting at your ankles and finishing up at your breast. Ohhh. Then repeating his tongue journey on your right side, you let out more than an ohh this time. All the while he is licking; his hands are no more than 1inch above your body to where you can only feel the heat from them.

Spreading your legs, he licks your shaven pussy just lightly enough to wake her up to the point she is up and looking around! Then without a hint and no hesitation, he grabs your legs by your ankles and plunges his tongue into your body. On that initial penetration, your legs shake as your body puts out a liquid welcome mat.

If he was to put his technique in writing it would be the NY Times Bestseller!!

With every lick and kiss he moves his head in directions to exemplify the feeling and as he is moving his mouth, his hands are pivoting your legs to present your body open and ready for his tongue lashing.

His tongue movement is sick! His tongue would go in and press against your walls putting sensual pressure in the right spots! Probing, caressing, touching you in ways you have only heard about or read in magazines. Your hands are fondling your breast with the same amount of intensity that he is licking your pussy! And when he sucks on your clit, you squeeze your nipples. You can't take it no more; you had to let out a lil squirt of appreciation.

Trying to move your legs but getting resistance cause of his strong manly hands grappling your ankles, you think it made it that much more exciting.

Feeling your body releasing, a thought hits your mind, "I know this man is not mine, lawd knows I know that! I know I need a man like him in my life on a more constant basis, but what am I going to do".

With a smack on your ass, you are brought back to reality, the land of the living and evidently the land of the cumming. While in a state of seductive bliss you lose control and started showering him with your moisture. Sensing and feeling your pleasure he comes up from below, and grabs your hands and guides your blinded folded ass into a position where you are now in the straddle position and lowering yourself down. You stop with great hesitation once you feel something touch my super exposed clit. If you had to guess, this mother fucker had you straddling his face! "Oh my god, what am I going to do with him?!?!"

Pulling you down, as his tongue, kiss, lips, and mouth grace you once again. Squatting with great balance and power, you hold your position and let him eat you in this wonderful position.

You feel your leg shaking, shaking and messing up your rhythm of movement against his tongue. You try to lift your body up, but his grip on your ass is so strong and domineering that you can't move. Succumbing to his will and pleasure you stay put knowing that any second now you are going to explode and this explosion is going to be the big one!!!

Just as your body starts to shout out satisfaction, he flips the script on you and pushes you down on your back with him on top of you. Then you feel it, you feel his manhood enter you; inch by inch the muscles in his dick stretch you out in a good and pleasurable way. Thinking to yourself, this beats any dildo you ever brought or have in your dresser draw now!!

As your body is still shouting, he is steady pumping away, making your body respond louder and louder with liquid shouts. With your hands, you grab your thighs and hold them up giving him absolute access to you. Knowing his sex game is tight, he works it out! He got his hips moving in such erotic ways that right after you finished letting loose, you feel your body firing off some more. Got you thinking, "this shit right here! This shit right is the motherfucking best it gets!!!"

Taking control of your legs he put them into an awkward setting; your right leg is lying flat on the bed while he got your left leg straight up in the air and this is all while your upper body is still lying flat on the bed. you never knew you was that flexible, it would take this good pussy eating fat dick nigga to bring out the best in you, huh? Now this new position did something to you, because every stroke he made now sent shock waves pulsing through your body; my mind was firing synapsis like crazy in the sensual part of your brain! You have already gave up on trying to keep count of the many times you came, so you were just along for the ride and let you tell it, this conductor knew how to ride.

He pulled out his wet dripping dick from all your ecstasy and helped you get into that supreme position of fucking, the doggy position! Blindfolded and reaching out to get a bearing on which way you are facing, you feel the wall, so you try to brace yourself with it. That helped only a lil bit, cause as soon as he put his dick back in you, your whole body shook something serious like you was having a seizure. He pulled out to let some of your over flow juices trickle down your inner thighs then he

stuck it back in you. Still shaking a bit from that

first plunge, you get control of yourself now.

Using the wall for leverage, you are pushing on it to

throw his ass back at him, trying to make sure you

get all of the feeling of his dick! With every push

you made he made a push deep into you. You were

silently praying for this to never stop! He heard you

whispering, that is when he pulled your hair with

the blindfold and whispered in your ear, "Is that

good to you?!" Without any hesitation, as if you

knew what he was going to ask, "Hell! Yeah!!

Please don't ever take this dick away from you!!"

You reached back with your right hand and started

to grip his thigh. Thinking you were overcome with

pleasure again and blacked out, cause in your

gripping of his thigh, you think you broke his skin digging your nails. Driving that dick harder, longer and stronger, you felt every inch, every muscle, every vein and every time his balls kissed your leaky pussy, oh the motherfucking feeling!

As your body is being subdued by this man and his WMD (weapon of mass destruction) you collapse on the bed shaking and convulsing. Then he laid on top of you with that WMD (Weapon of Mass Destruction) poking right through your wet thighs and making his way into you again. He slid in very easy thanks to your body producing all that damn juice that now has your bed soaked up. As he grabs hold of your hips, you feel his hands tighten, his moans are getting heavier, his rhythm is more forceful, and this man is about to cum! So to help him unload, you push your booty back and up giving it to him like he likes. As he is back there doing his thing, he got your ass squeezed together creating a new found friction from your lips hugging onto his dick as it slides in and out. Still not completely over that last orgasm he gave you, I feel something else coming.

Just as his body releases his warm, sticky, and milky white sauce within you, your body answers back with your cool, slippery and clear sassiness. The combination of your individual extracts happening within you sets your mind ablaze. The thought of the passion just mixing up with in your uterus has me lost in pure admiration that I just smile and shake your head.

Pulling his dick out, you can feel every inch as it slides out and your well satisfied hole says goodbye. But your body is still trembling and it now has an over flow of juices seeping out and traveling down to be deposited on the wet up sheets of lust.

You try to calm down by putting your hand in-between your thighs, but that does nothing to help. You just lay there and let it take you where it wanted to go. After your fit subsides, you fall asleep right there where you are. While you were sleeping, you didn't notice him get up, get dressed, clean up the living room or write you a note that he put on the fridge on his way out the door.

The note said, "I didn't want to wake you, but I enjoyed our night together. I cleaned up and took out the garbage with me. Call me later sweetheart.

Signed…..

Mr Wonderful"

Like it was said in the beginning,

"Even though we don't see each other as often as I would like, but when we do, it is nothing less than magical. I mean the sex is amazing! But it goes deeper, the way he touches me, the way he talks to me, he gives me so much attention that I truly feel as if there is no one else in the world!"

Now you have to get up and get things ready for your husband to come home from his overnight job.

Jet Lag

Running late it is now 7:28am. My flight leaves at 8:30am and I am just leaving the house, thank god my car service is already outside. Ok this ride to the airport is about, 25minutes that will leave me with a half hour to get through airport security. This is going to be one crazy ass trip to Detroit.

Getting to the gate with only 2minutes to spare, I board the plane and find my seat next to a pretty, unassuming, nice, thick, woman trying to take my aisle seat when she is supposed to be by the window. But after she sees me there in the flesh she moves to her right seat. I get settled in with my laptop bag under the seat in front of me and buckle down for the flight. Just before takeoff, my neighbor starts the small talk, the common verbal jousting, "where are you headed?", "business or pleasure?", and "how often do you fly?". As we engage in this light conversation, she reveals that she is going to Detroit for a wedding and that she is happy to being single. Ok that's cool.

At cruising altitude, the fasten seat belt sign goes off. I pull out my laptop and start writing a chapter for my new book while my neighbor sits there acting like she is not paying me any attention. Then her curiosity gets the best of her, she inquires, and I tell her I am writing a book. I then pull out my first book "Seductive Bliss" and hand it to her, telling her she should read "the Getaway" first. Just then the pretty stewardess, I think her name was Jessica, came with drinks; I asked for my cranberry juice. While reading, she is constantly putting her hand over her mouth and removing it in a gesture of shock, but not once tried to close the book at all.

Finishing that story she went on to read another 3 chapters. I completely got tied up in my writing to even notice she put the book down and was staring at me, haha.

About another 40 minutes left for the flight, she says she is going to the bathroom and as she gets by me she places a handwritten note on my laptop. The note said, "meet me in the bathroom, knock 2 times then 3times to let me know it is you.".

So after she disappears into the bathroom, I get up and make my way. Doing exactly what she wrote, she opened the door and let me in. Once inside, she asked me why I had her read that damn book.

Before I could even answer, she already had dropped to her knees, my zipper was undone and my dick in her hands heading for her mouth. What is this chick some kind of a magician and shit?! With my dick in her mouth, she started to hum, and then she was licking it as if it really was a lollipop. The bathroom isn't that big so while pressed in there with no room to squirm, she sucked and kissed my dick at over 20,000 feet in the air. This gave me a whole new meaning to "the friendly skies". As she sucked and kissed I just relaxed my head back and closed my eyes. She was going to work with no hands now. Her hands were too busy grabbing my thighs, my butt, my stomach and chest. As I braced myself with my left hand on the mirror with my back against the wall and my hand on her head, I bumped my body into her face as I released nothing less than hot sperm oil into her mouth.

Pulling out slowly some of me leaked from her lips and dropped and hit the floor. Wiping her lips she started stroking my hard dick planting lil petite kisses randomly all over it; all the while pulling down her sweat pants for immediate access. Standing up and turning around, I pushed her body into the other wall as I penetrated her, moaning from being pressed up against the wall, she got louder once I was in.

As I slide in more, I can feel her poking out her butt, trying to get all of me. I bend my knees to get better leverage as I push up and in deeper. With every move I make, I feel her hips move in an opposite direction to creating some good frictional force. Not caring any more if I fall, I grab both sides of her hips and squeeze as I ride, as I pump and bump.

Her moans now are getting a lil more passionate and a lil bit louder, so to quiet her down cause I am not done what I am doing, I mash her face more into the wall in such a way that my hand covers her mouth. With her sounds muffled, her face up against the wall and getting fucked from behind her body starts to shake. Not paying attention to what is going on around us, she accidently hit the sink handle and the water is turned on high. Turning off the water, she gets back into the swing of it, throwing back your ass and licking my fingers that covers her mouth. Putting my right forearm in the small of her back, I force an arch into her back as I dig deep, and go long. Feeling her use that kegel exercises, your pussy tightens around my dick and at the same time she lift up that leg and put it on the toilet. Oohhh, that feeling right there! I can feel my peak coming and coming fast.

She reached down and started to rub her clit and yelled out, "don't stop cause I am cummin!"

The pilot comes over the intercom to let everyone know that we are 10 minutes from the airport. So to finish up, I go harder and stronger as my dick leaves a stream of semen dripping from her. Pulling out, I wipe off with a wet napkin and put "him" back together.

As I leave the bathroom she stayed to get herself together, I returned to my seat, feeling fully relaxed.

At the restroom in the distance I hear a knock on the door and it is the flight attendant asking is everything ok as everyone needs to be in their seat for our arrival in Detroit. Opening the door still looking a lil flustered, she shuffled past her and made her way back to her seat next to me. As she sits down, I comment that I wasn't able to finish that chapter I was planning on completing, to which she replies back with, "well, I think I just gave you a new chapter for this book". Thinking to myself, yes you did!

As we touchdown and exit the plane, she gave me a kiss on the cheek and says, "Good bye and thank you for flying the friendly skies".

Checking In

Making my way to the ground transportation

section of the airport trying to get to the hotel, I pass

by that flight stewardess and we exchange a simple

but meaningful head nod.

Now about a half hour has passed as I arrive at the

hotel. The building looks truly like a short stay

motel instead of a chain hotel with lavish amenities

but nevertheless, I am only here for the weekend.

Checking in and settling in to my room, I make a lil

quip at the room number I was given, 112.

Changing clothes, cause I am already late for

today's morning session meetings, I find the

meeting room and slip into the back and just

observe what is going on before doing anything to draw attention to myself.

Watching all the big wigs conduct business as usual, I find a pair of eyes watching me; now where I am sitting way back in the corner is no reason for these eyes to be focused back here but for me. Throwing up my hands to signal, "what's up", I get back the signal saying, "you're late", I laugh and wave my hand.

I find the right time to make it to my seat when the presiding officer is introducing another big wig. Sitting next to the rest of the delegation from my home town, I nestle right on in. This is going to be a long day of meetings.

Lunch time comes and everyone disperses to get some grub. As I am walking to the front desk, I see a familiar face, and could it be? Why yes, it is the flight attendant from my flight. This time out of uniform, wearing some navy blue sweat pants and a pink top as she talks to the front desk guy. I make way over to her and jokingly say, "Are you following me? That is against the law in several of the states we crossed coming here from New Jersey you know?". She lets out a smile and tells me that this is the hotel where they spend the night at. Just then, one of my colleagues call me from across the room asking If I was going with them to get something to eat. So, not to be rude, I kindly explain, I did have to go but wanted to see her later on that night if her time permits.

She leans in and whispers in my ear, my room is 234; call me when you are done. Leaving her presence, I can feel her eyes burning a hole right into me from her staring. I leave the hotel and her sight on my way to lunch.

Coming back from lunch, I debated about playing hooky from the next 3 hours of meetings and finding the flight attendant, however I came here to be in the meetings, so yeah, I went.

After the meetings were over and the time had just passed 6:30pm, I ring her room number on the hotel phone asking if she has had a chance to eat yet.

Saying she ate already I went out with associates to Southern Fires to get some soul food.

Returning back to the hotel, I went to my room to shower up and get ready for my rendezvous with the stewardess. Texting her to let her know I am back and about to jump in the shower she reply back with. "What room are you in, I will be there in about 45minutes."

While taking a shower with that hot water feeling so good, I find myself so relaxed and focused on the night ahead, that I rub out a load of cum and just stand there watching as it hits the shower floor. Ohhhhh, thinking to myself, now that first one is out the way, she better be ready for the thunder I am bringing!

Dripping wet, I get out and dry off and lotion up, can't be ashy larry on the first fuck maybe the 3rd but not the first. With a little more than 15minutes left before her arrival, I get the room ready; IPOD playing my 'Seduction Bliss' playlist, KY Intense jelly under the pillow, condoms in the draw near the bed, bottles of water in the cooler, spritz of my Carolina 212 cologne and I sprayed baby oil on the small wall near the bed.

Exactly 45minutes, the actual time is 8:15pm and there is a knock on the door, I open it wearing some grey sweat pants and my white 'XXXPLEASURES: SEDUCTIVE BLISS' t-shirt. She enter the door way wearing her nicely fitted jeans showing off that sweet onion booty, a sweater top trying it's best to hold down them sweater puppies. I tell her how beautiful she is and how I like them jeans. She returns my compliment by grabbing my dick and pushing the door closed.

Ok, I see we are not playing fair huh, no problem, I didn't have any intentions on playing fair either.

Pulling up on that sweater, exposing her purple laced bra with the breast meat peering over top (I am not a breast man, but what a wonderful pair of C cups). With the top removed, I can't help myself but to kiss on her shoulder and as I am kissing them I am rubbing her sides and admiring her skin. Lowering my hands, I start un-buttoning her jeans, turning her around to navigate getting these jeans over that hump she is blessed with. I find myself starting at the base of her neck and licking down her spine right into the small of her back. Moving my head to the right side as I slide off; her shoes to allow her pants leg to come off as well I almost pass out from the sight of all that butt meat being contained in them fucking boy shorts!!!!

Now with her only in her underwear standing before me, my sweat pants are bulging. The sight is so beautiful and pure I feel just like a devil about to defile a pretty flower in all its glory.

She sits me down on the bed with her back to that small wall near the bed, the one with the baby oil on it. With me sitting there, she performs a lil strip tease winding and grinding on her imaginary pole with ease and skills. Turning her dance into a crowd participation, she drops down low and pulls my sweat pants off, revealing that I was free balling. Twirling my pants around her head like a trophy, she slings them across the room. Leaning to one side and popping that ass to the other side, she starts taking my shirt off while keeping her eyes totally fixated on what is between my thighs.

Now as I am completely naked, sitting and anxious the dance gets even raunchier as she gracefully removes her bra. Getting her eagle on, she makes them boy shorts disappear, and oh my god, the view of her beautiful body on display in front of me is something to behold.

Facing me she lifts her left hand and flicks her finger telling me, "to come here". Getting up with my dick just swinging, I grab her and pick her up and she wraps them damn lovely thighs around my waist and holds her body up as we interlock in a passion filled Hershey kiss!

Feeling it running through my body, I push her up against that oiled up wall and to her surprise, her body lowers and just like magic she is impaled with my dick that has been waiting to penetrate her silky flesh. On impact she damn near bit off my lip, she almost came from the initial feeling of this big dick poking inside of her.

Using the oil to slide up, down, side to side, she rides my body like she was born just for this one reason! Trying to brace herself from the explosion she feels coming into plays, but not able to cause the slippery walls got her going crazy! I continue to reach for the stars and only ending up tickling her heart. As her body let's out some pre-cum, she feels like she got to do something to either get in control of her body or change the tides on this situation.

She starts trying to bite me on my shoulder, but seeing that makes me pump harder and faster so she stops, I let her down and quickly spin her around to where her frontal body parts are now sliding along that oiled up wall as I'm holding her hips with one hand and my other forearm is pressed against her back between her should blades while I am deep in her again. The whole left side of her face is right now lightly coated in baby oil. Feeling the loss of body control she let out some more pre-cum.

With those deep, hard, long in and out movements, I see residue from her early juice flow. Trying to throw her ass back, she is greeted with fatboy at every throw back.

Pulling out, I turn her around and lay her down on the bed; no one is thinking about all that oil on her back. Positioning her legs, I got them spread and propped up with her feet flat on the bed. Feeling like a miner I go in deep with my tongue, I lick around in a circle while burying my face in between them thighs. With the palms of my hands, I clamp down on the underside of her thighs making her legs dangle in the air.

With no pattern just straight up random licking, I lick on her pussy and suck on her moist clit with such intensity and precision. She knew you had met her match now! With my tongue constantly pressing that button, her body releases a steady stream of pure satisfaction. Wetting up my chin, I back up a lil bit and use my finger to shake your clit while she is letting go.

As her flow subsides, I wipe my face and get back into it. There is a wrestling match going on with my tongue and her clit; right now her clit is losing. My tongue has it pinned into a submission hold. Her hands grab her knees to hold up her legs even more as I lay my fat tongue to her sweetness. Holding her knees is all she can do to keep her hands from pushing my head away from her in an act of weakness. With a strong right hand, I roll her body over guiding her up and onto her hands and knees. With my left hand I guide my dick enter her, I push into her til my ball are touching her wet dipping pussy. The warmth of her drippings glides down my sack and just drips onto the bed where her oiled body once rested.

Backing up she feels my thighs against yours. Just staying still she relishes at the thought of the sex-scapades we are having. Who would have known!?!?!

Feeling my hands gripping her hips, she prepares herself for this ride. With strong movements, I push her body away and she push it back at me. Back and forth, back and forth! Pushing her away til my dick head is just outside her sweet hole, she pushed back til my balls slap up against her pussy in repeated movements. Every time she bumps back, I throw a lil something extra into my thrust back to her. She feels what feels like my dick moving her stomach to the side. She feels what feels like her body being stuffed from the inside. While the riding gets more powerful and her breast are swaying with the forward and backward progression, her body start to tremble; her body start to liberate itself of her organic juices. Pulling out as her body is still pouring; I tease her clit with the tip of my dick.

Pushing her down on the bed, she collapsed and continues to shiver. Balling up in the fetal position her body is still dripping and shaking as the faint sound of, "ohhhhhhh" can be heard escaping her mouth. Lying next to her, she curls up around me like she is seeking warmth.

Reaching her hand up, she grabs hold of my dick an begins to lightly caress me. Feeling how stiff I am, she sits up and brings the other hand into the act. Now with both hands working hard, she lowers her mouth onto my throbbing dick head. That feeling right there is heaven sent!!!! With her eyes closed and me in her mouth, I just lay my head back and succumbed to her will and pleasure. As she goes to work on my dick I grab her head and commence to fucking her face. Holding her head as I work my dick in her mouth, my pelvic propulsion sends shock waves through her body. As her body grapples with the urge to release some more savory liquid I shout out words of fulfillment, "Shit!!, oh shit!!! Don't stop, suck that dick!!"

Coming from deep within my balls an eruption of great magnitude outburst from the head of my dick shooting up and in her mouth til she moves her head and let the warm sultry jism hit my stomach.

Holding my dick still she climbs up on top of me and she pops my dick in her and slowly lower her body down onto me. At the half way mark, she lifts up again with the head just prodding at her soaked pussy. With one hand still holding my dick and the free hand playing with her clit, she lowers down again. Feeling her playing, I lunge upward sending erotic jolts up and through her body. Trying to hold her body up at the half way point her body is rocked by one of those jolts of numbness to the point that she falls all the way down on my dick. Taking all of it at one time, her body launches into a fit of vibration.The next thing I know her body is blasting off into contentment.

With her moment passing, she finds energy from somewhere. Squatting over me, she lines up my dick and just drops down and bounces on it like she is possessed,. She is trying to take 'riding dick' to a new level with the sounds of her sweaty ass hitting my thighs and both of our sounds of passionate moans, groan and ahhs filling the room completely.

Bouncing on top of my dick she is riding like she is on a wild bull and she is trying to break him in! With her hands on my chest rocking back and forth, I feel her skin sliding up and down, riding my dick just right. Her nails are breaking my skin as she digs deep trying to hold onto her sanity while making mad passionate, unadulterated carnal sex. On every motion down taking in all of me within her, she turns her head and bites her upper lip. Grabbing her hands to stop her from truly drawing blood, we interlock fingers. I got a trick for her, pushing upward while pulling her hands downward I throw a lil swivel in my hips.

Feeling the motion, she starts to pivot, rotate, and twist them pretty hips of hers. Letting go of her hands, I scoop up her butt in my hands. The feeling of her round bottom in my grips helps solidify that feeling I was looking for. In an acrobatic move, I pull out and get right up behind her with her face smashed in an array of hotel pillows. Her arms are spread out as she just lays there and takes all of me. After several good long strokes, I pull out and begin to use my dick as a whip to beat her on her ass. Shoving my dick back in, I can feel her body releasing yet again.

Reaching my hand up, I grab a handful of her hair and tug it back towards me. As if on cue, her body challenges me, but to show who is in control, I pull back tighter and throw more dick. As my dick hurling got more and more concentrated I grew a hump in my back and went to town on her ass. Forcing dick all up in her, her legs began to shake, cumming all over my dick. I pulled out and got down low to suck the deposit of cum she was putting out while I jerked off and spilled all over the bed.

Becoming over ridden by a good orgasmic release, we both just collapse. My alarm is now going off telling me it is now 7:45am. Not caring about going to breakfast I hit the alarm clock like it hit me first. With peace and quiet in the room again, I dose off, while she got up, got dressed, kissed me on the forehead and left the room.

That morning, while I was running late for another round of meetings, I see her in the lobby loading her

172

bag on the airline van taking her and her colleagues back to the airport. Seeing her ride off, all I can think about is how nice her sexy ass was last night/this morning!!! During a break from my meetings I went back to my room and found a letter slipped under my door from my last night visitor saying, "Last night was great, I wish had more time, but I have to make a living. Til we see each other again, please keep fatboy thinking about me. Kathy 413-555-9201"

That night I slept like a baby all alone in my room, but I thought about her and the night before. For some reason I woke up with a load of my cum sitting on my right thigh..

Sexual Quotes....

I'm not cheap, but I am on special this week.

~Author Unknown

How lucky we are that we can reach our genitals instead of that spot on our back that itches. ~Flash Rosenberg

I'd like to meet the man who invented sex and see what he's working on now. ~Author Unknown

Kinky is using a feather. Perverted is using the whole chicken. ~Author Unknown

Don't worry; it only seems kinky the first time.

~Author Unknown

My sexual preference is often. ~Author Unknown

Bonus

Computer Love

Standing in the bathroom doorway as you are in the shower, I can't help myself but to think about your body as software and my body as hardware. I scan your body from head to toe bit by bit.

The beauty that you possess is sometimes too much for my central processing unit to comprehend all at once and I start to over flow my memory RAM chips.

Being together for as long as we have our love is a wonderful thing, the way our operating systems always seem to be in sync. As you step out of the shower I see a big drop of water rolling down your skin. Quickly with my tongue I catch that drop as it descends and gets close to your belly button.

Moving up I kiss on your right breast because it is visible and lit up like a LCD monitor screen. While showing some attention to your breast I find my fingers caressing your skin like keys of a keyboard.

The network connection right now between us is strong and feels like we are running 1Ghz of love speed. You got my hard drive spinning with heavy data traffic flow; I turn you around, bend you over and insert my DVD into your slim line optical drive. Watching as you compile all of code I can see that sweet look of pure satisfaction all over the printout you're producing.